Kevin Garnett

Revised Edition

By Jeffrey Zuehlke

AMAZING
ATHLETES

Lerner Publications Company • Minneapolis

Copyright © 2011 by Lerner Publishing Group, Inc.

Lerner Publications Company
A division of Lerner Publishing Group, Inc.
241 First Avenue North
Minneapolis, MN 55401 U.S.A.

Website address: www.lernerbooks.com

Library of Congress Cataloging-in-Publication Data

Zuehlke, Jeffrey, 1968–
    Kevin Garnett / by Jeffrey Zuehlke. — Rev. ed.
        p.   cm. — (Amazing athletes)
    Includes bibliographical references and index.
    ISBN 978-0-7613-5594-6 (lib. bdg. : alk. paper)
    1. Garnett, Kevin, 1976– —Juvenile literature. 2. Basketball players—United States—Biography—Juvenile literature. I. Title.
    GV884.G3Z84 2011
    796.323092—dc22 [B]   2009035645

Manufactured in the United States of America
2 – BP – 12/1/10

TABLE OF CONTENTS

Kevin Garnett scores two points for the Celtics during Game 6.

WINNING IT ALL

Boston Celtics' head coach Doc Rivers called for a **time-out**. His team was losing to the Los Angeles Lakers. They were playing Game 6 of the 2008 National Basketball Association (NBA) **Finals**. Boston had already won three games in the series. If they could win Game 6, they would be the NBA champions.

Boston **forward** Kevin Garnett knew that his team would have to play better **defense** to win the game. "The defense is our backbone," said Kevin. He and his teammates were up to the challenge. Kevin jumped to grab **rebounds**. He soared through the air to **block** shots.

The Celtics' efforts paid off. By **halftime**, Boston had the lead, 58–35. Lakers' star Kobe Bryant knew that his team was in for a fight. "They were definitely the best defense I've seen the entire **playoffs**," Kobe said.

Kevin plays tough defense against the Lakers' Pau Gasol during the first quarter of Game 6.

Kevin and the Celtics didn't slow down in the second half. Boston player Paul Pierce made shot after shot. Kevin grabbed more rebounds. The crowd roared around him. Boston won the game, 131–92. The Celtics were NBA champions!

With this victory, the Celtics had won the NBA championship for the 17th time. This is more than any other team in NBA history. But 2008 marked the first championship for Kevin and his teammates.

Paul Pierce (center) shoots over Lakers' players Ronny Turiaf (left) and Kobe Bryant (right).

Kevin holds the NBA championship trophy.

The Celtics celebrated on the court after the game. With the crowd cheering and cameras clicking, Kevin could relax.

After the Celtics, the Los Angeles Lakers [15] and the Chicago Bulls [6] are the next teams on the list of NBA champions.

After years of hard work, he had finally reached the top. With tears streaming down his face, Kevin looked to the sky and shouted, "Anything is possible!"

A Gift for the Game

Kevin Garnett was born on May 19, 1976, in Greenville, South Carolina. His mother, Shirley Garnett, worked in a factory. Kevin has two sisters, Sonya and Ashley.

Kevin's father, O'Lewis McCullough, didn't live with Kevin's family. Kevin didn't see his father much, but they shared one thing. Both of them loved basketball. O'Lewis had been a great player as a young man. Kevin soon showed he had a gift for the game too. Kevin played basketball as often as he could.

In 1988, when Kevin was 12 years old, the Garnetts moved to Mauldin, South Carolina.

Jaime "Bug" Peters *(left)* first met Kevin when they were neighbors in South Carolina.

Kevin's neighbor across the street, Jaime "Bug" Peters, also loved basketball. Kevin and Bug became best friends. They spent most of their free time on the basketball court.

By this time, Kevin was growing fast. He was already taller than most of the kids his age.

As a kid, Kevin's favorite player was Magic Johnson of the Los Angeles Lakers.

Being tall helped Kevin to beat other kids in **pickup games**. He could shoot over other kids and block their shots. He could even jump high enough to make slam dunks.

In 1991, when Kevin entered Mauldin High School, he was six feet seven inches tall. He was a natural for the school's basketball team, the Mavericks. Kevin dreamed of playing for a big-time college team or even in the NBA.

Kevin wore number 21 when he played for Mauldin High School. He was a lot taller than most of the other players.

Kevin played with energy and emotion in high school.

ALL-AROUND PLAYER

Basketball is a team sport. To win, every player has to do his or her job. Kevin understood this. He always tried to give his teammates chances to play better. He wasn't a ball hog. Instead, he passed the ball to the teammate who had the best shot. Kevin's style made the Mavericks a winning team.

Kevin moved to Chicago, Illinois, in 1994. He led Farragut Academy's Admirals to a winning season.

In 1994, Kevin and his family moved to Chicago, Illinois. For his senior year in high school, Kevin went to Farragut Academy. He soon became the basketball team's star player. With Kevin leading the way, the Farragut Admirals won 28 games and lost only 2. Kevin averaged 28 points per game.

By this time, basketball experts were calling Kevin the best high school player in the country. All the big college basketball programs wanted him. But to get into these programs, Kevin had to pass a college test. Taking tests made him nervous, and he got bad scores.

Yet Kevin had another choice. Some basketball experts said Kevin was good enough to skip college and go straight to the NBA. Others said this would be bad for Kevin because he was too young. Kevin thought he could make it in the NBA. He decided to try to enter the NBA **draft**.

Before the draft, Kevin showed off his skills for NBA teams. Throughout June 1995, he played in several practice games called scrimmages.

NBA scouts and coaches loved Kevin's skills. The Minnesota Timberwolves wanted Kevin on their team. They chose him as the fifth pick in the 1995 draft.

Kevin was going to play against the world's best basketball players. Was he good enough to win against them?

Kevin was the first player in 20 years to go straight from high school to the NBA.

Kevin shows his serious focus during a game against the Los Angeles Lakers in 1995.

DA KID

Kevin began his **rookie** season in November 1995. The Timberwolves knew Kevin had a lot to learn. So they didn't put too much pressure on him. For the first half of the season, Kevin spent a lot of time on the bench. He watched and learned. He played just a few minutes every night.

Kevin learned fast. He practiced hard. And the Wolves' coaches and fans liked him. Kevin was always smiling and having fun. Because he was so young, people called him Da Kid. The nickname stuck.

By the second half of the season, Da Kid was in the starting lineup. He blocked shots and grabbed rebounds. He threw down thunderous slam dunks.

Kevin's spectacular slam dunks entertain fans.

In his first season, Kevin shows off his ball-handling skills in a game against the Miami Heat.

Kevin made the NBA All-Star Team in only his second season. At 20 years old, he was the second-youngest All-Star ever. That same season, the Wolves had drafted talented **point guard** Stephon Marbury. Stephon's speed and shooting skill gave the Wolves two star players.

Stephon Marbury brought a spark to the Wolves in the 1996–1997 season.

Kevin charms a Japanese fan at an off-season basketball camp.

Kevin and Stephon led the Timberwolves to their first-ever playoff appearance in 1997.

By this time, Kevin had become one of the NBA's most popular players. Fans all over the world were wearing his number 21 Timberwolves jersey. They loved how he played hard and always had a smile on his face. They cheered his powerful slam dunks.

Kevin talks with reporters after signing a huge new contract to stay with the Minnesota Timberwolves.

The Timberwolves wanted to keep Kevin on the team for a long time. During the summer of 1997, the team offered him a new **contract** that was worth $126 million! Kevin signed the deal. The big contract earned him a new nickname—the Big Ticket. Thousands of Timberwolves fans were buying tickets to see Kevin play.

Kevin faces off against forward Tracy Murray in 1997.

Kevin gave his best effort in the 1998 playoffs against the Seattle SuperSonics.

THE BIG THREE

Kevin worked hard to earn his money. The Wolves made the 1998 playoffs. They played tough but lost in five games.

Kevin and the Timberwolves had some problems in the 1998–1999 season. Stephon said he didn't like playing in snowy Minnesota. So the Timberwolves **traded** him to the New Jersey Nets.

The next four seasons, Kevin and the Wolves continued to play great basketball. They made the playoffs four years straight. But each year, they faced better and stronger teams. The Wolves always came up second best.

Before the 2003–2004 season, the Wolves traded for Latrell Sprewell and Sam Cassell. With Kevin, Sam, and Latrell leading the way, the Wolves stormed through the regular season. They won more games than any NBA team in the Western **Conference**.

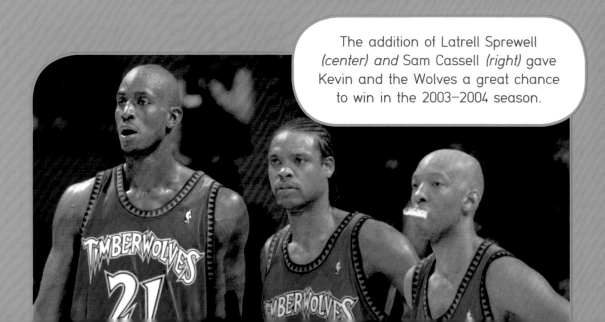

The addition of Latrell Sprewell *(center)* and Sam Cassell *(right)* gave Kevin and the Wolves a great chance to win in the 2003–2004 season.

Kevin had a monster season. He led the league in total points and total rebounds. To top off the season, he was voted the NBA's Most Valuable Player (MVP).

The Timberwolves were a good team and had hopes of winning the NBA Finals. But Kevin and the Wolves came up short against the Lakers in the Western Conference

Kevin holds up the 2004 MVP trophy. The award goes to the year's best player in the NBA.

Finals, losing four games to two. He and his team would not get to play in the NBA Finals.

The next three seasons were hard for Kevin and the Timberwolves. Sam and Latrell both left the team. Without much help for Kevin, the Timberwolves missed the playoffs for three straight seasons. Minnesota didn't seem to be getting any better. They were far away from Kevin's dream of winning the NBA Finals.

After the 2006–2007 season, the Wolves made a very hard decision. They needed to figure out a way to make the team better. Minnesota decided that they would have to trade Kevin to another team. In return, the Timberwolves would get a group of younger players. These younger players would be less expensive than Kevin and might grow into stars someday.

Before the start of the 2007–2008 season, Minnesota traded Kevin to the Boston Celtics. The Wolves received five players, two draft picks, and money for their superstar forward.

Kevin was sad to leave Minnesota. But he also knew that going to Boston was a great chance. "This is probably my best opportunity at winning a [championship]," Kevin said. The Celtics already had two superstars in **guard** Ray Allen and forward Paul Pierce. Kevin, Allen, and Pierce became known as the Big Three.

Ray Allen *(left)* and Kevin *(right)* run a play against the Memphis Grizzlies.

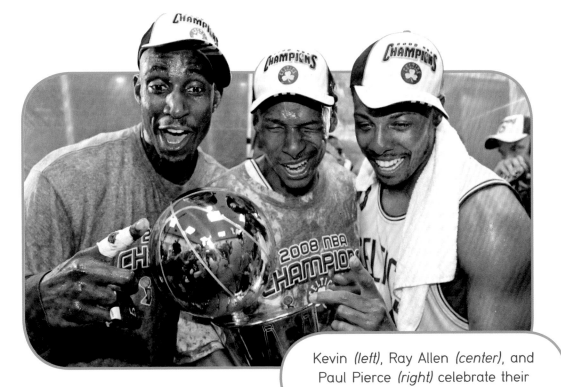

Kevin *(left)*, Ray Allen *(center)*, and Paul Pierce *(right)* celebrate their 2008 championship.

The Big Three helped the Celtics to the best record in the NBA for the 2007–2008 season. They rolled to the NBA Finals and defeated the Lakers in six games. After the big win, Kevin talked to Bill Russell. Russell had won championships with the Celtics in the 1950s and 1960s. "I hope we made you proud," Kevin said to the Celtics' legend. "You sure did," Russell replied.

Kevin hurt his knee during the 2008–2009 season. Boston made the playoffs, but Kevin's sore knee kept him from playing. The Celtics lost to the Orlando Magic in seven games.

Kevin and his Boston teammates will never forget their NBA Finals victory. But with the Big Three on the team, the Celtics are hoping to create even more championship memories in the years to come.

Kevin goes up for a dunk at the beginning of the 2009–2010 season.

Selected Career Highlights

2009–2010 Named to NBA All-Star Game for 13th time

2008–2009 Named to NBA All-Star Game for 12th time

2007–2008 Won NBA Championship with Boston Celtics

2006–2007 Led the NBA in rebounds per game
Led the NBA in **double-doubles**, with 66

2005–2006 Led the NBA in rebounds per game
Led the NBA in double-doubles, with 62

2004–2005 Led the NBA in rebounds per game
Led the NBA in double-doubles, with 69

2003–2004 Voted NBA MVP
Led the NBA in total rebounds
Led the NBA in total points scored
Led the NBA in double-doubles, with 71
Became the first player to be named Player of the Month four times in one season

2002–2003 Voted NBA MVP of the 2003 NBA All-Star Game
Named to All-NBA First Team

2001–2002 Selected to fifth NBA All-Star Game
Named to All-NBA Second Team

2000–2001 Selected to fourth NBA All-Star Game
Named to All-NBA Second Team

1999–2000 Selected to NBA All-Star Game
Won gold medal as member of the U.S. basketball team at 2000 Olympic Games in Sydney, Australia

1998–1999 Named to All-NBA Third Team

1997–1998 Voted as starter to his second NBA All-Star Game

1996–1997 Selected for NBA All-Star Game

1995–1996 Named to NBA All-Rookie Second Team

1994–1995 Named National High School Player of the Year by *USA Today*
Named Mr. Basketball of Illinois, as the best player in the state
Played in the 1995 McDonald's All-American Game

Glossary

block: to stop another player's shot from going in the basketball hoop

conference: one of the two groups of teams in the NBA. The groups are the Western Conference and the Eastern Conference. The winner of the Western Conference Finals meets the winner of the Eastern Conference Finals in the NBA Finals.

contract: a written deal signed by a player and his or her team. The player agrees to play for the team for a stated number of years. The team agrees to pay the player a stated amount of money.

defense: plays that try to stop the other team from scoring

double-double: making ten or more contributions in two categories in the same game. For example, a player who makes 10 points and 12 rebounds has a double-double.

draft: a yearly event in which professional teams in a sport are given the chance to pick new players from a selected group

finals: the last set of games in the NBA playoffs. The winner of the NBA Finals is the best team in the NBA for the season.

forward: a player on a basketball team who usually plays close to the basket. Forwards need to rebound and shoot the ball well.

guard: a player on a basketball team whose main job is to handle the ball. Guards need to be good passers and good shooters.

halftime: the break in the middle of a basketball game

pickup games: casual games, not run by a league or organization

playoffs: a series of contests played after the regular season has ended

point guard: a player on a basketball team who directs the other players and who handles the ball most of the time

rebound: grabbing the ball off the hoop or the backboard after a missed shot

rookie: a player who is playing his or her first season

time-out: a period when play is stopped for a short time during a basketball game. In the NBA, each team gets six time-outs per game.

trade: to exchange a player on one team for a player on another team or for other benefits